Hairy Maclary
from Donaldson's Dairy

Lynley Dodd

TRICYCLE PRESS
Berkeley, California

Out of the gate
and off for a walk
went Hairy Maclary
from Donaldson's Dairy

and Hercules Morse
as big as a horse

with Hairy Maclary
from Donaldson's Dairy.

Bottomley Potts
covered in spots,
Hercules Morse
as big as a horse

and Hairy Maclary
from Donaldson's Dairy.

Muffin McLay
like a bundle of hay,
Bottomley Potts
covered in spots,
Hercules Morse
as big as a horse

and Hairy Maclary
from Donaldson's Dairy.

Bitzer Maloney
all skinny and bony,
Muffin McLay
like a bundle of hay,
Bottomley Potts
covered in spots,
Hercules Morse
as big as a horse

and Hairy Maclary
from Donaldson's Dairy.

Schnitzel von Krumm
with a very low tum,
Bitzer Maloney
all skinny and bony,
Muffin McLay
like a bundle of hay,
Bottomley Potts
covered in spots,
Hercules Morse
as big as a horse

and Hairy Maclary
from Donaldson's Dairy.

With tails in the air
they trotted on down
past the shops and the park
to the far end of town.
They sniffed at the smells
and they snooped at each door,
when suddenly,
out of the shadows
they
saw . . .

SCARFACE CLAW
the toughest Tom
in
town.

"EEEEEOWWWFFTZ!"
said Scarface Claw.

Off with a yowl,
a wail and a howl,
a scatter of paws
and a clatter of claws,
went Schnitzel von Krumm
with a very low tum,
Bitzer Maloney
all skinny and bony,
Muffin McLay
like a bundle of hay,
Bottomley Potts
covered in spots,
Hercules Morse
as big as a horse

and Hairy Maclary
from Donaldson's Dairy,

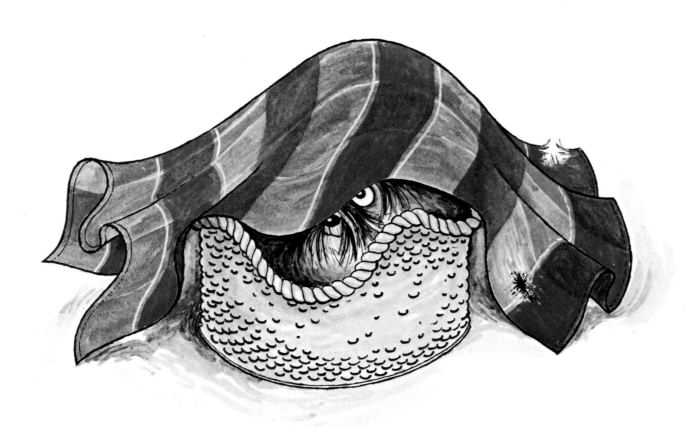

straight back home
to bed.

Other TRICYCLE PRESS books by Lynley Dodd
Hairy Maclary and Zachary Quack
Hairy Maclary Scattercat
Hairy Maclary's Bone
Hairy Maclary's Rumpus at the Vet
Slinky Malinki
Slinky Malinki Catflaps
Slinky Malinki, Open the Door

TRICYCLE PRESS
an imprint of Ten Speed Press
PO Box 7123
Berkeley, California 94707
www.tricyclepress.com

Library of Congress Cataloging-in-Publication Data
Dodd, Lynley.
Hairy Maclary from Donalson's Dairy / Lynley Dodd.
p. cm.
Summary: A small black dog and his canine friends
are terrorized by the local tomcat.
ISBN-13: 978-1-58246-059-8 / ISBN-10: 1-58246-059-0
[1. Dogs—Fiction. 2. Cats—Fiction. 3. Bullies--Fiction.
4. Stories in rhyme.] I. Title.
PZ8.3.D637 Hai 2001
[E]--dc21

2001027612

First Tricycle Press printing, 2001
Printed in China

5 6 7 8 9 — 12 11 10 09 08